ATTACK OF THE DROWNED

ATTACK OF THE DROWNED

AQUATIC ADVENTURES IN THE OVERWORLD

BOOK TWO

AN UNOFFICIAL MINECRAFTERS NOVEL

MAGGIE MARKS

Sky Pony Press
New York

AQUATIC ADVENTURES IN THE OVERWORLD:
ATTACK OF THE DROWNED.

Sky Pony Press books may be purchased in bulk at special discounts for sales promotion, corporate gifts, fund-raising, or educational purposes. Special editions can also be created to specifications. For details, contact the Special Sales Department, Sky Pony Press, 307 West 36th Street, 11th Floor, New York, NY 10018 or info@skyhorsepublishing.com.

Sky Pony® is a registered trademark of Skyhorse Publishing, Inc.®, a Delaware corporation.

Visit our website at www.skyponypress.com.

10 9 8 7 6 5 4 3 2 1

Library of Congress Cataloging-in-Publication Data is available on file.

Special thanks to Erin L. Falligant.

Cover illustration by Amanda Brack
Cover design by Brian Peterson

Paperback ISBN: 978-1-5107-4728-9
E-book ISBN: 978-1-5107-4739-5

Printed in the United States of America

TABLE OF CONTENTS

ATTACK OF THE DROWNED

CHAPTER 1

"Are you sure you don't want to make these walls stronger?" asked Luna. "You could make them two blocks thick." She tapped against the glass.

Mason sighed. They'd already spent days building his new underwater home. Hours melting sand in the furnace to make the last few blocks of glass. And the last forty-five minutes sopping up the remaining water from the floor with sponges.

"Nope," he said. "Those walls sound plenty thick to me. Besides, I like to be able to *see* through them."

He gazed out at the underwater ruins of the sandstone village he now called home. A crumbling, moss-covered fountain stood tall, gazing at him like a friendly neighbor. Sea grass waved hello from the coral reef beyond. And a tropical fish stopped to peer through the glass before darting toward its school of friends.

Luna chewed her lip. "Well, remember that every mob down here can see *you*, too," she said. "You probably should have used the tinted-blue glass, like I have in my house."

"Every mob?" said Mason. Sure, he'd battled plenty of mobs when he and his brother, Asher, lived above ground. But down here, the world seemed more peaceful. "You mean like the turtles and the fish? I'm not worried." He glanced again out the window, just in time to see a long black tentacle reach up from the ocean floor and tap on the glass.

Mason jumped backward and dropped his sponge with a *splat*. Then he recognized the sleepy eyes of Luna's pet squid.

"Edward! Stop sneaking up on me like that!" scolded Mason.

Luna laughed. "You've got to watch out for those squid," she said. "They're such dangerous mobs."

"Well, don't forget the dolphins," joked Mason as he bent to pick up his sponge. "I hear they're deadly."

Luna nodded with mock enthusiasm. "Yes, especially if you attack one of them," she said. "Then they'll turn on you like zombie pigmen. Or like . . ."—a shadow passed over her face—"the drowned."

Mason's stomach clenched. He'd been trying to forget about the zombie-like mobs that lived on the ocean floor. But he knew Luna couldn't forget. She had lost her parents in a drowned attack right here in this underwater village.

He quickly changed the subject. "Maybe I should have used the tinted glass. But you should be glad I built this house instead of Asher. He pretty much wanted us to live in that pile of dirt over there."

He pointed at the mound just beyond the crumbly fountain. A wooden door was nailed to the front of the mound, with the smallest of rooms dug out behind it. That's as far as Asher had gotten in his "building" before moving on to something else.

Luna chuckled. "What's he doing out there now?" she asked, pressing her face to the glass.

Mason looked, too. Redheaded Asher was standing next to a coral tree, stacking blocks of prismarine. "He's trying to build a conduit power structure," said Mason. "Except without a conduit."

"Huh?" asked Luna.

"It's what Uncle Bart sketched in his journal, remember?" Just saying his uncle's name made Mason's heart sink. He and Asher had been traveling with Uncle Bart, until their ship overturned in a storm and tossed Uncle Bart into the raging waters.

Mason shook off the horrible memory and pulled his uncle's leather journal from his pocket. He flipped to the right page. "See?" he said. "Check it out."

Uncle Bart had sketched a square base of prismarine, five blocks wide and three blocks tall. In the center, he'd drawn a conduit, crafted from nautilus shells and the heart of the sea. When the conduit was activated, Uncle Bart had told them, it would make it easier to breathe underwater, to see and mine underwater, and even to attack hostile mobs.

"Uncle Bart was making a plan for us to live underwater all along," said Mason. "He was searching for that heart of the sea when he . . ." His voice cracked. "Well, he never found it. But Asher hopes *we* can someday."

Luna nodded. "We will," she said. "I'll help you." She swept her dark bangs off her forehead and gazed again through the glass. "Looks like Asher is just a couple of blocks short."

Sure enough, Asher seemed to be scanning the underwater village for more prismarine. He pulled his pickaxe out of his backpack and then glanced back at the house.

"There's not a lot of prismarine around here," said Luna. "Can he use other blocks instead?"

Mason studied the scrawled notes in Uncle Bart's diagram. "It says here that sea lanterns work, too," he said. "Prismarine and sea lanterns." He gazed up at the lanterns that cast a warm glow throughout his new home.

But outside the glass walls, shadows were forming. Night would be falling soon.

"Asher should come inside," said Mason. "It's getting dark, and his potion of water breathing is going to wear off any minute now."

"It's alright," said Luna. "He's holding his breath for a lot longer now, and he's a stronger swimmer, too."

Mason nodded. When they'd first joined Luna down here, Asher could barely do more than doggy paddle. But living underwater had strengthened his muscles and his lungs. *Mine, too,* thought Mason.

Still, he was glad when Asher started swimming toward the glass house.

"I'm going to dry out these sponges in the furnace," said Mason, hurrying toward the hall. "You know Asher will bring a bunch of water inside with him."

They had built a flush entrance, a double front door that would let Asher swim through one door and then close it before opening the next. A sponge mat would soak up all the extra water—or at least most of it. But Asher wasn't very good at waiting for that to happen.

Mason plopped the wet sponge in the furnace and then returned to the living room. He expected Asher to burst through the door any moment now, shaking off water like a wet wolf.

But he didn't.

Instead, Mason heard a faint tapping coming from overhead. Or was it from behind? He spun in a slow circle, trying to find the source of the noise.

Luna cocked her head. "I think Asher is mining," she said.

"He found a sea lantern?" Mason wondered aloud.

"Maybe. But you can't mine lanterns—not without the silk touch enchantment."

Mason swallowed hard. "Yeah, I don't think he knows that."

The tapping grew louder. With each blow, the glass walls rattled.

"He's really close by," said Luna, worry creeping into her voice.

"Too close," said Mason, his throat tight. "*Way* too close."

He'd barely gotten the words out when he heard the *snap* and *crack* of glass.

And then water began gushing in.

CHAPTER 2

Mason darted out of the path of the waterfall, trying to find its source.

"There!" Luna pointed toward a glass block—or toward where a block used to be—in the upper right-hand corner of the room. "Grab something to plug it up!"

Mason slipped and slid across the floor, searching for something. He grabbed the first thing he could find: a block of dried kelp from a stack near the furnace. Then he stood on tiptoe to force it into the hole.

The water gushing through the hole pushed back.

"Help me!" cried Mason as water streamed down the front of his shirt.

Luna stood beside him, pressing too. Finally, the kelp block gave way—just enough to fit. Then it swelled with water, sealing the leak.

"Asher!" Mason bellowed, hoping his brother could hear him even beyond the glass walls. "You're in big trouble!"

He couldn't storm outside and scold his brother, at least not without suiting up first. By the time he'd grabbed a helmet enchanted with respiration, he'd calmed down just a bit. And as he reached for a pick-axe, he made a plan.

Asher had destroyed one of his building blocks. So he would take one of Asher's in return.

Mason stepped out into the watery world and swam—no, strode—toward the conduit power source. Asher was nowhere to be found. *Probably hiding in a patch of kelp,* thought Mason.

He raised his axe and whacked at a prismarine block, which fell to the ground. Then he carried it toward his new house, stopping to admire the view from this side of the glass. The walls were shiny and perfectly clear—except for the ugly block of dried kelp stuck through the cracked hole.

Mason waved at Luna through the glass, pointing toward the dried kelp. Then he pointed toward his prismarine block. Luna nodded. She stood beneath the kelp with a sponge, ready for the water that would stream in as Mason switched out the blocks.

On the count of three, thought Mason. He held up his fingers, one at a time.

On *three,* he destroyed the kelp block with a whack of his axe. Then he quickly pushed the prismarine block into place. It wasn't clear glass, but it was strong—and much more attractive than the kelp.

Luna mopped up the water inside with her sponge, pausing only to give him a thumbs-up through the glass.

Then someone grabbed Mason's arm from behind. He whirled around and came face-to-face with . . .

. . . a very angry Asher. He pointed up at the prismarine block as if to say, *That's mine!*

Mason shrugged. Then he swam toward the front door, knowing that Asher would follow.

When they were dried off and sitting inside, Mason explained. "I took your block because you destroyed mine—and you almost destroyed our house, too. You have to be more careful when you mine, Asher!"

His brother threw out his arms. "I'm sorry!" he cried. "But I'm really close to finishing the conduit power source. I mean . . . except for actually having a conduit." His shoulders slumped. "We need to find the heart of the sea."

Mason sighed. Asher was so much like Uncle Bart, always in search of buried treasure. "Can't we just enjoy our new home for a while?" Mason asked. "We have practically everything we need, right here in this village."

Luna nodded. "Plenty of kelp to eat—and to burn as fuel."

"A roof over our heads," added Mason, "that we can see right through!" Through the gallons of water overhead, he could see the shimmer of the moon.

"And good friends," added Luna with a smile.

But the corners of Asher's mouth drooped. "Sure," he said glumly. "We have everything we need—except the heart of the sea."

In the silence that followed, Mason and Luna exchanged a glance. Then Luna straightened up. "So we'll find it," she said. "I have a buried treasure map. You do, too—your Uncle Bart's. Between the two maps, we ought to be able to find *something*, right?" She stood up and dusted off her hands, as if she'd just solved all of the Overworld's problems.

Asher jumped to his feet. "So we're going then?" he asked.

Luna laughed. "Well, not right this second. We should probably wait until morning. And we need to do a few things first, like enchant our tridents. The ocean is *crawling* with drowned. We need to be ready."

Mason shivered. He and Asher had fought off their share of the undead mob in the past few weeks.

"The drowned are everywhere," Asher agreed. "*That's* why we need to build the conduit. For protection!"

Mason couldn't argue with that. "We'll build it. We'll find that heart of the sea," he promised. "Maybe even tomorrow."

* * *

"Mason, wake up!"

It seemed as if Mason had just laid down on his red wool blanket, and now Asher was shaking him awake. Morning sunlight streamed down through the glass ceiling above.

"What?" asked Mason, running a hand over his tousled blond hair. "What do you want?"

"I can't find Luna!" said Asher.

Only then did Mason realize that Asher's hair was

wet. A droplet landed on his arm, sending a shiver through his body. "You've been out already today?"

Asher nodded. "Luna's not at home."

Mason sighed and wiped his arm dry. He pushed himself up on one elbow. "She's probably enchanting the tridents, remember?"

"But where?" asked Asher.

Mason hesitated. He'd been in Luna's house plenty of times. She had a furnace, a couple of chests, a crafting table, and a brewing stand. But he'd never seen an enchantment table or an anvil.

"I don't know," he said. "She's probably using an anvil somewhere else in the village. She'll be back soon." He stifled a yawn. "Want some breakfast?"

Asher shook his head. "I'm not hungry. I want to find Luna so we can get going." He stared at Mason with a look that said, "I'm not going to leave you alone until you help me."

Mason sighed. "Fine. Let me get dressed and we'll go together."

Fifteen minutes and a fried cod breakfast later, the boys were swimming through the village. As Asher swam ahead, nimble as a fish in the water, Mason shook his head in amazement. Was his brother going to sprout fins soon?

Mason felt the strength of his own legs as he kicked to catch up. When the boys had first met Luna, Mason had marveled at how long she could hold her breath. Now, he could do the same, thanks to his enchanted helmet and weeks of swimming through the ocean.

Up ahead, Asher darted past a moss-covered castle. It wasn't a *real* castle, but it was the tallest building in the village, with a gravel floor and a sea lantern casting welcoming light on the crumbling staircase nearby. Some of the houses surrounding it were a maze of connecting rooms. Others were nothing but roofless huts melting into the ocean floor, remnants of what used to be.

When Asher darted through an open window, Mason called out a gurgly warning. Then he saw Asher pop out the other side. The window was carved into a single standing wall. The other three walls had toppled to the ground long ago.

Asher passed through another sandstone arch before he turned around. He held up his hands, as if to say, "Where is she?"

Mason shrugged. Which of these buildings might hold an enchantment table or anvil? He had no idea.

Then his eyes caught a flicker of light up ahead. He swam past Asher and waved for him to follow.

The light seeped out through a crack in a stone wall. As Mason peered through the opening, he sucked in his breath.

The crack led to a large cavern. Inside, a girl was brewing a potion, colored liquids fizzing and bubbling up out of her cauldron. *Luna?* he wondered for just a moment. But as his eyes adjusted, he could see now that it was a woman, not a girl. Her hair was much longer than Luna's and flecked with gray.

As she turned toward him, his heart pounded in his

ears. They locked eyes for just a moment before Mason pulled away from the crevice.

But Asher had caught the expression on Mason's face, and now he wanted a look of his own.

Mason reached for his brother's arm, but it was no use.

Asher pressed his face toward the crack. By the time he pulled away, his jaw was set, which meant he was determined to learn more. He turned toward the opening to the cave. Then, with a swift kick, he was gone.

No! Mason wanted to holler. *Don't go in there! We don't know if she's a friend or an enemy!*

But Asher had already disappeared through the opening, and Mason had no choice but to follow.

A short tunnel opened up into the cavern, lit by a sea lantern and the bubbling potion in the brewing stand. The woman standing over the cauldron lifted her head. Her lined face tightened with surprise. She raised a bony finger, pointing toward the entrance. Then she pushed off from the rocky ledge and began to swim toward them, her white robes flowing behind her.

Mason grabbed Asher's arm and pulled him backward.

Swim! he wanted to shout. *Now!*

Finally, Asher turned to leave. But would he be fast enough?

Mason glanced over his shoulder and saw the woman swimming toward them, fast as a drowned.

Her mouth had tightened into a grimace, and her eyes flashed with anger.

CHAPTER 3

S*wim!* Mason urged again, pushing his brother out of the cave ahead of him.

With each stroke, he imagined those bony fingers grabbing his shirt, yanking him back toward the dark depths of the cave. Who was this witchlike woman? And what did she want with them?

He swam faster, not wanting to find out.

Past the stone arch, past the single wall of the ruined building, toward the castle-like structure with the sea lantern. There, at the top of the stairs, stood Luna, holding a trident in each hand.

She wasn't staring at Mason. She was staring *behind* him. With a jolt, Mason realized that the old woman must be right on his heels. He panicked, kicking faster and pulling Asher forward.

Luna waved the brothers toward the steps. Then she pointed down toward the bottom of the staircase. Mason half-swam, half-crawled down the steps, making sure his brother was close behind. When he reached the bottom, he flung open the wood trapdoor and squeezed into the flush entrance. As soon as Asher was inside, they pulled the door shut.

In the darkness, Mason waited for Luna to join them. Where was she?

When the water had soaked into the sponge at Mason's feet, he shivered in his damp clothes. He pressed his ear toward the outer door, listening for Luna. But when he saw Asher's teeth chattering, he pushed through the next door, hoping the ruined castle held a furnace so that they could dry off.

The stone corridor that stretched out before them was lit with torches. Mason blinked, wondering how they stayed lit during flooding. *Maybe this place doesn't flood,* he thought, reaching out to stroke the sturdy stone walls.

He and Asher followed the tunnel down and to the right, where it opened up into a larger room. An anvil sat in the corner. *Mystery solved,* he thought, glancing at Asher. *This is where Luna does her enchantments!*

But where *was* Luna?

When she finally burst through the door behind them, she didn't look scared. But she didn't look happy either.

"What were you doing back there?" she hollered.

Mason raised his hands, feeling guilty but not knowing why. "Did she follow us?" was all he could say.

Luna's brow furrowed. "No, but she should have! Why were you trespassing in old Ms. Beacon's cave?"

Ms. Beacon?

Asher didn't look the slightest bit guilty. "She had a treasure chest," he announced.

"No she didn't," said Mason. "I didn't see one."

Asher stuck out his chin. "It was half buried in gravel, but I saw it—on the floor, behind her cauldron." He sounded kind of proud of his detective work.

Mason shrugged. It was possible that she had a chest, he guessed. He'd been so freaked out by the old woman—er, Ms. Beacon—that he hadn't had a chance to look around the cave.

"She was brewing potions, too," said Asher. "Is she a witch?"

Luna laughed out loud. "No, of course not. I brew potions, and I'm not a witch, am I?"

He shook his head.

"But Ms. Beacon brews much more powerful potions than I do," Luna admitted. "My parents told me once that she knows how to brew lingering potions, made with dragon's breath. And she even knows how to cure a zombie villager."

"A what?" asked Mason.

Luna's face darkened. "A zombie villager—a villager who is killed by a zombie or a drowned, but then . . . turns into a zombie himself."

Mason's chest tightened. He'd heard enough. "So you know Ms. Beacon?" he asked.

Luna nodded. "Yes. I mean, no—not really. But she's lived here as long as I have, probably even longer. She doesn't speak. She keeps to herself. And she *doesn't* like visitors."

"Sorry," said Mason. "How were we supposed to know?"

Luna's face softened. "You weren't. But now you do. So don't go back," she warned, looking mostly at Asher.

"But she has a chest!" Asher protested. "Do you think it has the heart of the sea in it?"

Luna shook her head so hard, her wet hair slapped against her cheek—and stuck there. "She doesn't. That was probably a loot chest, like mine, not a buried treasure chest. Stay out of it, okay?"

She stared at Asher hard.

Asher shrugged. "Okay. Don't worry about it. I'm no thief." He shot Mason an irritated glance. "Not like my brother, who goes around stealing prismarine blocks and stuff."

Mason was so deep in thought, he almost missed the jab. *Why would Ms. Beacon live alone in such a dark cave?* he wondered. *Why didn't she want visitors? Didn't she ever get lonely?*

Clink, clink, clink! The sound of the anvil jolted him out of his thoughts. Luna was already enchanting one of the tridents.

"Is that mine?" he asked, seeing the purple glow radiating off his weapon.

She nodded. "Now it has the riptide enchantment. If you throw it underwater, it'll propel you forward, too. Cool, right?"

He reached for the weapon, but Asher beat him to it.

"Very cool," said Asher, holding the heavy trident out in front of him.

Then Luna pulled another enchanted book from her backpack and slid it into the anvil, beside her own trident.

"Which enchantment is that?" asked Asher, pointing toward the book.

Luna smiled. "Loyalty," she said. "I'll never lose my trident again. It'll come right back to me after I throw it."

That could come in handy, thought Mason, wondering if Luna's enchantment was even better than his own.

"Let's try them out!" cried Asher, already rushing toward the door.

"Wait!" called Luna. "I have one more enchantment to do." She pulled Asher's small pickaxe from her pack and slid it into the anvil, along with another enchanted book. "Silk touch," she said. "So you can mine sea lanterns without destroying glass houses." She grinned.

Asher scowled, but as soon as she handed him the glowing tool, he gave Mason back the trident and admired his new axe.

"So we're ready?" Mason asked Luna.

She took a deep breath. "Yep. As ready as we're going to be."

* * *

By the time they'd made the swim back to their underwater base, Asher had mined a sea lantern with his enchanted pickaxe. He'd lugged it home and stacked it onto his conduit power source. Then he held up his pointer finger in the air, as if to say, "Only one more block to go."

Mason gave him a thumbs-up and then waved him toward their house. They had only half an hour to pack up before Luna would join them for their buried treasure adventure.

Inside, Mason tucked dried kelp and fish into his backpack. But Asher hadn't followed him back in yet. He strained his ears, hoping to hear Asher coming through the front door.

When he finally did, Mason met him in the living room, which was now covered with puddles. The prismarine block threw a shadow across the wet floor. But when Mason glanced up, he saw that the block *wasn't* prismarine anymore. It was sandstone.

"Asher!"

"Huh?" His brother glanced up with a look of innocence.

"Why did you do that?" Mason pointed toward the sandstone.

Asher shrugged. "I needed the prismarine."

Mason wanted to argue, but there was no time. A knock on the door told them that Luna had just arrived in the entryway.

"That block had better hold up," said Mason. "If our house floods again, you're going to help me clean it up."

Asher nodded. "It'll hold up," he said. "Don't worry about it."

Easy for you to say, thought Mason as he flung open the door to let a wet Luna inside.

"Ready?" she asked. "Let's plan a path." She unfolded her buried treasure map.

"So here's us." She pointed to the white dot at the bottom of the map. "And here's the treasure." She pointed to the red X at the top. The rest of the map was blank, except for a few outlines of land masses and structures.

Mason recognized an ocean monument in the middle of the map. He winced, seeing how far they'd have to swim. "Do we have enough potions to last?" he asked.

She nodded. "We have a couple of turtle shell helmets and some enchanted armor, too. I think we'll be fine."

I think? Mason didn't feel reassured by her words.

"So we'll swim around the ocean monument, not through it." She glanced at Asher, giving him her "don't mess around today" look.

He stared at the ceiling, whistling, as if to say, "Who, me?"

"As long as we avoid the monument, we won't run into any guardians," Mason reminded Asher. He shivered, thinking about the ugly fish mobs that guarded the monument's treasures.

"Right," said Luna. "The only mobs we'll have to worry about are the drowned. And if we swim high enough, toward the surface of the water and the sunlight, we won't have to worry about them either."

Mason tried to remember the last time he'd been at the water's surface—or on land. It seemed like ages ago that he and Asher had left their wrecked ship on the beach and taken the rowboat out into the water.

Our rowboat. That's it! thought Mason.

"So I just thought of another way to avoid the drowned," he announced.

Luna glanced up from her map. "I'm all ears," she said.

"We'll take the rowboat!" said Mason. "The one we anchored just above the village. It'll be a faster way to cross the ocean toward the treasure."

Asher nodded enthusiastically. "Let's do it!"

Luna hesitated. "I'm a faster swimmer than I am a rower," she said.

"Maybe *you* are," said Mason. "But as for Asher and me? I'm not so sure. And what if we find lots of loot we want to bring back?"

She nodded thoughtfully. "Alright. But don't get your hopes up. The rowboat might not even be there anymore. A lot can happen in the Overworld . . . when you're not looking."

She smiled, but Mason could feel the warning in her words. What *would* they find at the water's surface, after weeks of being down here?

A trickle of excitement ran down his spine. *Time to find out.*

CHAPTER 4

G*lub, glub, glub . . .*

Mason rose skyward in the bubble column, straight toward the morning sun. As he shot out of the water's surface, he could feel the warmth on his back. The bright sky blinded him. He closed his eyes and inhaled deeply, smelling land.

Then he remembered.

Mason turned toward the island, toward the shipwreck that he and Asher had once called home. He could see its splintered mast, rising high above the sand. But the rest of the ship looked broken and tired, even from a distance.

Something broke the water's surface nearby. As Mason spun around, he saw Asher pop out of the bubble column. Then he saw something else—a small rowboat bobbing a few feet away.

Our rowboat, thought Mason. *It's still here!*

Asher swam toward the side of the boat and grabbed hold, catching his breath before pulling himself over the edge. Mason climbed in, too, trying not to rock the boat. He had just settled himself on a seat when Luna popped out of the water.

Her eyes widened. "The boat's still here," she said, wiping the water from her eyes. But she didn't sound nearly as excited about that as Mason had been.

He chuckled to himself. Luna was part fish—more comfortable in the water than above it. But when he offered her a hand to help her into the boat, she took it.

"Can I hold the map?" asked Asher. "I'll be the navigator."

Luna hesitated. "Alright," she finally said, "as long as you promise not to lose it." She slid the folded map out of her pack.

"Awesome!" Asher grabbed the map and waved it like a victory flag.

"Stop!" cried Mason, reaching for his brother's arm. "It's windy up here. You'll lose the map before we even pull up anchor."

Asher settled down, but Mason couldn't help thinking that giving Asher the map had been a bad idea. "Which way?" he finally asked his brother.

Asher studied the map. "I don't know yet," he said. "Start paddling, and I'll tell you if we're going the right way."

Luna shaded her eyes as she glanced toward the sun. "The sun rises in the east," she said. "So . . ."—she spun a quarter turn to her left—"that's north. Go that way."

Huh, thought Mason. Asher might have been holding the map, but Luna was definitely navigating.

As they rowed the boat north, something sprang up from the water beside them. A dolphin! It bobbed its snout and squeaked at Mason before diving back down.

When it surfaced again, a second dolphin had joined in.

"There are three!" said Luna. "A whole pod—look!"

Sure enough, a family of dolphins had surrounded the rowboat. They dipped and dove playfully through the water, as if to say, "Yes! That's the way!"

By the time the dolphins had moved on, the map in Asher's lap had begun to fill in. "I think we're right over the ocean monument now!" he said. As he leaned to look over the edge, the boat rocked.

Luna gripped the edges of the boat. "Careful," she warned, "or we'll end up *in* the ocean monument." But she peered down into the water too. "I've never seen the monument from up above before."

Mason took a break from rowing to gaze down at the monument. He'd been in the monument once, exploring its maze of rooms and tunnels. But from up above, it looked so . . . well, perfect. Like a perfect square, with a rectangular entrance cut out of one side. And it looked *huge*. Minutes later, they were still passing over the top.

"What's next?" Mason asked his brother. "Anything interesting coming up ahead?"

Asher smoothed out the map. "Maybe an underwater village. I can't tell."

Sure enough, they were soon passing over the

crumbly remains of another village. "Do you think anyone lives there?" Mason wondered aloud. The thought of other people living underwater, not far away, gave him a rush of excitement. Then he remembered Ms. Beacon—and that excitement turned to dread. She'd been so unwelcoming. *So if no one lives in this village,* he thought, *that's fine by me.*

He rowed in silence for a while, until Asher began shifting in his seat. "We're getting close now," he said. "The red X is straight ahead!"

Mason studied the horizon, as if the buried treasure would suddenly rise out of the sand and present itself.

"Do you think the treasure will be on land, or buried underwater?" asked Asher.

Luna shrugged. "Probably on land," she said. "Most buried treasure is on land, I think. But you never know."

"Wait, what's that? Is that a fire?" Asher pointed at the low bank of clouds drifting across the water. A dark plume rose up from the horizon to greet them.

"It's smoke, alright," said Luna. "And where there's smoke, there's fire."

And where there's fire, there are probably undead mobs, burning in the morning light, Mason realized. *And more ready to spawn . . .*

He swallowed hard. "Maybe we should go back."

"No!" cried Asher. "What about the treasure? What about the heart of the sea?"

The brothers turned toward Luna, who had the deciding vote. She chewed her lip. "Someone could be in trouble," she said. "Let's go a little farther and see."

So Mason kept paddling. But with each stroke, the pit of dread in his stomach grew bigger.

He glanced down at the trident resting on the floor of the boat. He had the unsettling feeling that he was going to need that weapon soon. *Very* soon.

* * *

By the time they'd rowed ashore the small island, Mason could see that the plume of smoke was coming from several small fires. The island was dotted with them. But Asher was already leaping out of the boat, clutching the map in his hand.

"Careful!" Mason warned him. "There could still be mobs roaming around."

"Yeah, yeah," said Asher. "There could also be a buried treasure right under our nose." He reached into the boat for his enchanted pickaxe.

"Let's stick together," said Luna. She hopped out of the boat, too, and then reached back in for her trident.

As Mason took his first steps ashore, his legs felt wobbly, as if he were still in the boat. And his body felt so *heavy.* At the ocean's floor, he'd been fighting to keep his legs on the ground while the water pulled him upward. Here, on land, the earth was pulling him down.

Asher seemed to feel it, too. Normally, he'd be scampering around the island like a wolf pup. But now, each step seemed labored—until he checked the map. "We're really close!" he declared. "C'mon!"

When Asher took off like a shot, Mason struggled to follow. He darted around a burn pile and then stepped into something wet. And squishy. The smell wafted up to greet him.

Rotten flesh.

"Yuck," he said, dragging his foot in the sand to wipe it clean.

"Watch your step!" called Luna with a grin. But a second later, she was standing in her own pile of steaming flesh. "Ew!" she cried. "It's everywhere!"

Mason studied the sand between him and Luna. Sure enough, the beach was littered with zombie drops: rotten flesh, carrots, and potatoes. "What's going on here?" he asked, afraid to take another step.

Luna's face fell. "Zombie siege," she said. "I've seen this before, and . . . it's not good."

"But they're gone now," said Mason, "right?" He swung his head side to side, just to be sure.

Luna nodded, but the cloud on her face hovered, as if a storm were brewing.

Luna knows something I don't know, Mason realized. He was about to press her for information when he heard a yelp from up ahead.

"Asher!" Mason cried. He took off at a sprint, dodging burn piles and zombie drops. He raised the trident at his side, ready for battle. *Let me get there in time,* he pleaded, willing his heavy legs to move faster.

He caught sight of Asher just over a sand dune. He was kneeling beside something, but what? A dead mob? A critter? A zombie drop?

When Mason reached his brother, he leaned over, trying to catch his breath. "What is it? Are you hurt?"

Asher shook his head and pointed.

There, poking out of a smoldering burn pile, was the edge of a box. *No, not a box,* Mason realized. *It's a chest. A treasure chest.*

But instead of brown wood, the chest had turned ash black.

Asher had finally found his buried treasure, but that treasure had been burned to a crisp.

CHAPTER 5

"Don't touch it!" Luna cried as she skidded to a stop in the sand. "You'll burn yourself."

The treasure chest did look hot to the touch—and fragile, as if it would disintegrate the second someone tried to open the lid.

"Is it ruined?" Asher whimpered.

Yes. Definitely. Without a doubt, Mason wanted to say. But Asher looked as if he might fall to pieces any second now, too, so Mason stayed silent.

Together, they dribbled cool ocean water over the chest until it stopped smoking. Then they dug it out from the sand and dragged it into the open.

"Do you want to do the honors?" Luna asked Asher, nodding toward the chest.

Asher looked torn, as if half of him was dying to know what was inside the treasure chest, and the other half was dreading seeing all that glorious loot burned to a crisp.

Finally, he reached out his hand and nudged open the lid.

The smell hit Mason before anything else. *Fish. Blackened fish.* Asher grabbed it with his fingertips and flung it into the sand with disgust.

Below that was a leather tunic, charred and tattered. And a half melted iron sword. As Asher lifted it out of the chest, the nose of the sword pointed downward, bending into an upside-down U.

"Oh, man," he said, glancing back into the chest. "Is that what I think it is? I can't even look."

So Mason looked for him. Sure enough, the last thing in the chest was a round black ball. The heart of the sea.

As Mason reached for it, the treasure disintegrated into a pile of ash.

"No!" Asher wailed. "We came all this way!"

Luna sighed. "Just be glad there wasn't any TNT in this chest," she said, "or we all might have been blown sky-high."

Leave it to Luna to always look on the bright side, thought Mason. But his own spirits had sunk like an anchor to the ocean floor.

He glanced around the island, hoping there'd be something else here to make the journey worthwhile. "Look," he said, pointing. "Should we check that out?"

A small hut stood a few yards away, a curl of smoke rising from its roof. "Maybe there's a furnace inside," said Mason. "Or even a supply chest with food." His stomach rumbled at the thought. He and Asher had eaten nothing but dried kelp and fish for weeks now.

"Food?" said Asher, lifting his chin. "Like . . . bread? Or potatoes? Or mushroom stew. Ooh, mushroom stew!"

He jumped to his feet as if the heart of the sea were now a distant memory.

"Wait," said Luna, "there could still be mobs inside."

"Right," said Mason. "Let's go together."

But Asher was always a step ahead. He got to the hut first and swung open the door, with nothing but a pickaxe at his side.

Then he took a giant step backward.

Something grunted, and groaned, and staggered out of the hut. A zombie!

Mason swung into action, raising his trident. But he couldn't throw it—Asher was in the way.

"Run!" Mason cried.

But Asher wasn't a runner. He was a fighter. He swung his pickaxe, knocking the zombie backward toward the hut.

Luna threw her trident, striking the mob in the chest. It tumbled downward with a groan.

But more zombies were spilling out of the hut. Two, three, four . . . How many could it hold?

Mason didn't have time to count. He raced toward the hut, his weapon raised, until Luna held up her hand. She pointed toward the sun, and then Mason realized. They didn't *have* to fight. The morning sun would do it for them.

Sure enough, the mobs began to sizzle. And moan. And burn.

"Get back!" Mason cried to Asher, who was standing too close to one of the undead mobs.

As the creature burst into flames, Asher yelped. The sleeve of his T-shirt flickered with flames.

In an instant, Mason had knocked his brother to the ground. He forced Asher to roll in the sand, trying to smother the fire. Finally, the flames were out. Asher's sleeve had turned black and smoky.

Then Mason heard a grunt from over his shoulder.

As he glanced backward, he caught the stench of the undead mob. A zombie staggered toward him. Why wasn't it burning? As a cool shadow spilled across the sand, Mason had his answer. The sun had slipped behind a dark cloud.

Then Luna was on the mob, swinging her trident like a sword. As Mason pulled Asher out of the way, Luna knocked the zombie backward toward the waves. He took one more staggering step back, and then another, until he fell with a horrific splash.

Below him, Mason felt Asher squirm. "Get. Off. Me!" Asher grumbled. "I'm fine!" But as he sat up, he held his injured arm.

"Put some cool water on it," called Luna, waving him toward the water—away from where the zombie had fallen.

While Asher crouched in the sand, dipping his arm in the waves, Luna dropped her trident. She pulled off her backpack and rummaged through it. "Potion of healing," she muttered. "It's here somewhere."

Finally, she pulled a vial of sloshing pink liquid from the depths of her pack.

Asher reached for it, ready to take a swig, but Luna shook her head. "It's a splash potion," she said. She uncorked the potion and jerked the bottle forward, drenching Asher with the liquid.

"Hey!" he cried. "Watch it!" He wiped his face.

Mason laughed out loud. "You should be relieved!" he said. "At least you didn't have to drink something nasty."

Luna used some pretty disgusting things in her potions, like fermented spider eyes and fish oil. But her potions always worked. Asher was already moving his arm in a slow circle, as if it were feeling better.

Then he froze. And pointed.

"What?" asked Mason. He followed Asher's gaze down into the waves, where the zombie had taken its last step. But the zombie wasn't gone. It hovered just below the water. And it was shaking, sending ripples toward the surface above.

"What's happening to it?" Asher cried.

"I don't know," said Mason. "Get back!" He pulled his brother onto the sandy shore.

But Luna stepped forward. As the zombie began to push itself out of the water, she uncorked her potion again and splashed the mob.

"What are you doing?" cried Asher. "Trying to heal it?"

"No!" cried Luna. "Potion of healing doesn't heal zombies. It harms them."

Sure enough, the mob fell backward, snarling.

By the time it rose again from the waves, Luna was ready. She threw her trident like a spear, knocking the zombie back underwater—for good.

As the mob disappeared, its tattered brown robes swirled round and round. "Wait, that wasn't a zombie," Mason cried. "That was a drowned!"

"No," said Asher. "It was a zombie."

Luna held out her hand, waiting for her enchanted trident to return. It snapped out of the water and back into her palm, ready for battle. "It was both," she practically whispered.

"What?" asked Mason, wondering if he'd heard her correctly.

She faced him, her eyes wide. "That zombie just turned into a drowned."

Mason sucked in his breath. He'd heard about things like that happening, but had he just actually seen it with his own eyes? "Well, at least you got it," he said. "Nice job with the trident!"

But Luna didn't look relieved. She looked horrified.

"How many more zombies from that siege have already turned?" she asked. "How many drowned are swimming right now, heading toward our village?"

Mason felt a trickle of dread run down his spine. He'd just built their glass house underwater. He didn't want anything to happen to it. *Or to us,* he thought with a shudder.

Luna knew a thing or two about zombie sieges and drowned attacks. So when she began packing up the boat and pushing off, Mason quickly followed. "Get in," he told Asher. "Let's go."

Mason paddled back in the direction they had come from, faster and faster, hoping to beat any drowned back to their underwater base.

No one said a word. In the silence, Mason heard every stroke of the paddle in the water and felt every lurch forward. He held his breath, as if a drowned might suddenly surface and reach its gnarly hand toward the boat.

At the very thought of it, Mason paddled harder. Faster. The wind picked up, carrying them forward with each gust. But when they'd reached the middle of the ocean, Mason could no longer tell where he was going.

"Asher," he called over his shoulder. "We need the map. Which way do we go?"

Asher sat up, as if coming out of a deep sleep. "Right," he said. "Let me grab it." He dug deep into his pocket, and then into the other one. As his hands came up empty, fear flickered across his face.

"I don't have the map," he said. "I must have lost it—back on the island!"

Mason groaned. "Do we need to go back for it?" he asked Luna.

She heaved a great sigh. "Back where?" she asked.

As Mason spun around, his stomach sunk. The island had disappeared. They were surrounded by a sea of blue, without a map.

A thick layer of dark clouds hung overhead, which

meant there was no sun to guide them. And as a droplet of water splashed onto his cheek, and then another, Mason realized something else.

A storm was brewing.

CHAPTER 6

The raindrops turned into sheets of wind and water. As the boat rocked side to side, Mason's stomach tossed and turned with it.

"Hang on!" he hollered to Asher. But his voice was instantly sucked up by the wind.

Asher clung to the edge of the boat, his eyes wide.

Is he remembering what I'm remembering? Mason wondered. That horrible night on the ship, when Uncle Bart had ordered them below deck. *But how could we go?* thought Mason. *He needed our help!* So the brothers had stayed on deck and seen Uncle Bart's last moments, when the ship had lurched sideways and sent their uncle toppling into the waters below.

Mason squeezed his eyes shut, trying to forget.

Then he forced them back open. *We need to stay strong,* he reminded himself. *We can't freak out!*

Luna had kicked into action, too. She'd pulled a compass from her backpack and was holding it up toward the dark sky. "That way!" she hollered, pointing. "We need to paddle west. No, southwest."

But she was pointing directly into a storm cloud! And now the wind was circling around, pulling the boat backward instead of forward.

"Help me paddle!" Mason cried to Asher.

Together, they took one long, strong stroke. But as Mason pulled the paddle up out of the water—just a few inches to give Asher more to grab—the wind took it right out of his hands.

The paddle tumbled backward off the boat and into the raging water.

Asher went after it. By the time Mason reached his brother, all he could grab were his sneakers. The rest of his body hovered just above the churning waves.

"Hang on!" cried Mason.

With Luna's help, he pulled Asher back in. But the boat shook violently now, with no one at the oar. With no oar at all. And water had begun to slosh around Mason's feet.

"What do we do?" he cried. His teeth chattered uncontrollably.

Luna held her voice steady. "We dive," she said solemnly.

"Into the water?" asked Asher, voicing the question Mason had wanted to ask.

She nodded. "It's calmer down below than it is up here. We have no choice."

As she pulled a potion from her soaking-wet backpack, Mason recognized the blue liquid: potion of night vision. The world underwater would be dark and shadowy. Luna struggled to pull the cork from the slippery-wet bottle, and then she handed it to Mason. As the boat lurched, he got a double dose of the carrot-flavored liquid. He coughed and handed the bottle to Asher.

The next potion—the sweet, sugary potion of swiftness—was easy to drink. But the last one, potion of water breathing, was not. The fish-flavored liquid tasted nasty, but Mason held his nose and forced it down. His new worst fear wasn't the boat sinking. It was running out of air underwater. He made sure Asher got a solid drink, too, before handing the bottle back to Luna.

Please let us get home safely, Mason whispered to the stormy skies. *No zombies. No drowned. And plenty of potion to get us there.*

He strapped on his turtle shell helmet and stepped to the side of the boat. The wind nearly knocked him off his feet, but he hung on—waiting until Luna had jumped into the stormy sea.

"Your turn!" Mason hollered to Asher. "I'll go last."

Asher plugged his nose, as if he could keep the water out, and jumped.

Here goes nothing, thought Mason. As a crack of lightning lit up the sky, he followed his brother off the side of the boat.

After being soaked with cold rain, Mason welcomed the warmth of the water. And Luna was right—the water under the surface was much calmer. Down,

down, down he dove, quick as a dolphin chasing its pod. The potion of swiftness had kicked in. Mason could feel it coursing through his limbs.

Luna led the way with her compass, past the remains of an underwater village. Here, every moss-covered building was graced with a sandstone arch. The edges of the huts were rounded, smoothed by years of ocean waves. Tropical fish darted in and out of windows, flicking their tails at Mason as if telling him to move on, that this village belonged to them.

He studied their tiny faces and fins, lit by potion of night vision. *That means the potion of water breathing must have kicked in, too,* Mason realized. He stopped holding his breath and inhaled deeply, letting the water cool his lungs.

As he followed Asher toward the glow of a sea lantern, Mason felt his body relax. His worries began to wash away. Sea grass tickled his arms and legs as he hugged the ocean floor.

When a squid lifted its lazy head, Mason didn't even flinch. This little guy looked just like Edward, Luna's pet squid. Mason patted the creature on the head, gently so that it wouldn't squirt him with black ink, and then swam onward.

But as they neared the ocean monument, Mason sensed a change in the world around him. The water felt cooler in the shadows of the humongous structure, and darker, even with potion of night vision.

Luna kept checking over her shoulder, a sure sign that there was potential danger ahead. So Mason swam faster, matching strokes with Asher, until they were side by side.

Stay close, Mason told Asher with a look.

As they approached the prismarine pillars, Mason glanced up, wondering if he could see the top. But the monument was endless—it seemed to stretch to the sky itself.

Faster and faster Luna swam, as if she were in a hurry to pass by the structure. Mason was, too. But Asher reached out his hand, letting it glide along the smooth turquoise-colored blocks of each pillar.

Stay away from those! Mason wanted to holler. He waved to get Asher's attention.

Guardians could be hiding behind the pillars: hostile fishlike mobs with orange spikes and thrashing tails, mobs that could blast Asher with a laser before he even knew what had hit him.

When Asher suddenly stopped swimming, Mason sucked in a mouthful of saltwater, wondering what his brother had seen.

Then he saw it, too—a menacing shadow.

Something lurked behind one of the pillars. A guardian? No, this wasn't a fish mob. This mob had a torso and legs.

Mason watched in horror as the drowned stepped out from behind the pillar. It staggered forward like a zombie, then turned and stared, its tattered brown robes rippling in the water.

Mason hung suspended, unable to look away. The mob's eyes were so blue and *so* cold.

Then in an instant, those eyes flashed and the mob lunged forward.

Protect Asher! thought Mason. He grabbed his trident and stepped in front of his brother.

The drowned was close now—mere feet away. With every ounce of strength Mason could muster, he swung his trident.

Whack!

It knocked the drowned backward. But it slowly crawled to its feet.

Whack!

The drowned hit the stony ground again with a grunt.

As Mason stood over the undead mob, waiting for the slightest movement, something flickered in the corner of his eye.

Asher? No, his brother was on his other side.

Mason whirled to his right, ready to take on another drowned. But . . . which one?

The prismarine pillars of the ocean monument had come to life, wriggling and writhing with mottle-skinned mobs.

Mason wasn't facing another drowned.

He was facing a whole *army* of them.

CHAPTER 7

The drowned spilled out of the ocean monument, climbing over one another to get to their prey. *To get to us,* Mason realized.

"Swim!" he hollered to Asher, bubbles gushing from his mouth.

He wanted his brother to get a head start, to swim away while Mason fended off the first few drowned. But Mason knew better—Asher wouldn't leave him behind.

So together they fought.

Mason swung his trident against the first drowned. *Whack!* The drowned staggered backward as if in slow motion.

Asher darted toward the next drowned and then away, as if taunting the mob. When it followed, Asher swung his pickaxe. *Thwack!*

Then Luna was beside the brothers, too, launching her trident like a spear against the wave of drowned.

The first few mobs grunted and groaned, falling

one by one. Their drops littered the ocean floor. When a pile of hot rotten flesh rose toward Mason, he swiped it away with his arm.

Luna was behind him now—he saw the flash of her trident. Wait, no . . . He glanced again.

The trident was sharp and shiny. But a *drowned* carried the trident, not Luna!

As it released its weapon, Mason dove—just in time. The trident zipped over his head, tunneling through the water. But seconds later, the drowned was holding another trident.

Mason darted left and right, like a fish in a net. *I can't get away,* he realized. *There's no escape!*

He ducked, waiting for the next blast. But it never came.

As the drowned dropped in front of Mason, he saw something sticking out of the mob's shoulder—Luna's trident. Then she was tugging Mason's arm, urging him forward.

What's the use? he wanted to holler. *We're outnumbered!*

But she didn't want him to fight. Luna pointed at the trident in Mason's hand and then motioned for him to throw it—*away* from the drowned that were creeping ever closer.

Then Mason remembered: his trident was enchanted with riptide. He'd been using it like a sword instead of like a spear. But if he threw it . . .

He instantly raised his hand and released the trident. As it tunneled through the water, his body lurched forward, following his weapon. He zipped through the water without even swimming. Without a single stroke of his arms or kick of his legs. He was flying!

But wait! he suddenly realized. *What about Asher?*

As he grabbed his trident, he slowed down—and then whirled around. The drowned had become a writhing mass of green and brown. Was Asher somewhere in the middle of it all?

Mason threw his spear again, aiming carefully to the side of the mobs. His body lurched and he was beside his trident in a flash, searching for Asher.

Luna waved to get his attention and then pointed. Asher was behind a pillar, backing away from a drowned. He raised his pickaxe, but the weapon looked so small!

Before Asher could attack—or *be* attacked—Mason swam toward him and grabbed his hand. He glanced back at Luna, who nodded, as if to say, *Go! I'll be right behind you.*

So with his other arm, Mason threw his trident—fast and far away. He held tight to Asher's hand, taking his brother with him as they zoomed after the trident. Again and again he threw his weapon, following it home.

He glanced back only once, hoping Luna would be behind them. But all he could see was the endless ocean. Dark murky water stretched out for miles.

Will the drowned follow us home? Mason wondered. *Or . . . are they already there?*

* * *

"I've never seen so many," said Luna as she wrung out her hair by the furnace. "Well, not since . . . last time."

By "last time," Mason knew just what she meant. The last time the drowned had overtaken the village. The last time Luna had seen her parents alive. He swallowed hard.

He and Asher had made it home safely, and then waited for what felt like hours for Luna to show up, too. They'd beaten the drowned back home. But Mason knew the mobs would show up soon. He could feel it, like a tentacle of dread wrapping around his body, making it hard to breathe.

"Are you dry yet?" he asked Asher, who sat huddled near the furnace.

His brother nodded, but his teeth were chattering. "If we'd f-finished the conduit," he said, "the drowned w-wouldn't come here. They'd s-stay away."

"I know," said Mason. "You did your best. But you can't finish it without the heart of the sea."

As he reached for another block of dried kelp to add to the furnace, he saw how low the supply had gotten. "We should stock up on fuel," he said. "Just in case."

Luna nodded. "Good idea. I have plenty at my house. I can bring some food back, too."

As she stood to leave, Mason felt his stomach twist. He hated to see Luna go. If the drowned *did* show up, he and Asher would need her help fighting them off.

"Let me check our food supply first," he told her. He crossed the room toward the chest. As he lifted the lid, his shoulders slumped. Two cooked cod fillets rested next to a single bunch of fresh kelp.

Not good, thought Mason. If he and Asher still lived above ground, they'd have potatoes. Loaves of bread. Mushroom stew. But down here, they relied on fresh fish and kelp.

So that's it, he realized. *I have to let Luna go out for more food.*

He handed her a helmet and followed her out of the furnace room. But as soon as Luna reached the glass-walled living room, she stopped.

"What is it?" asked Mason. "Did you forget something?"

She raised a finger to her lips and pulled him forward.

The living room, which was usually filled with light, felt dark and shadowy. But why?

Mason stepped around Luna and instantly froze.

The clear glass walls were lined with mobs. The drowned pressed their mottled faces to the glass, peering in with their ice-cold eyes. One of the mobs began to bang on the glass.

Thump. Thump. Thump.

Each blast rattled the glass.

Thump. Thump. Thump.

Mason's heart pounded in his ears.

Thump. Thump. Thump.

"What is that?" Asher cried, racing into the room. He stopped short. "Uh-oh."

"Uh-oh is right," whispered Luna. "We're in trouble now."

Mason had never heard Luna use those words before. "What do we do?" he asked.

She shrugged. "We wait," she said. "We hope they go away on their own. Before . . ."

"Before what?" asked Asher.

"Before we run out of food," she said. "Or fuel. Or water."

Mason nearly laughed out loud. "We're surrounded by water," he said. But Luna was right. How would they bring any water inside to drink? How could they step outside—without getting attacked?

Thump. Thump. Thump.

As the walls shook, Mason held his breath, hoping the walls he had built were strong enough. His throat tightened with worry.

"Let's go back to the furnace room," he said, trying to hold his voice steady. "Maybe if they can't see us, the drowned will go away." What he really meant was, *Maybe if I can't see them, I'll be able to breathe again.*

As they headed back toward the furnace, Mason reached for another block of dried kelp, hoping that a blazing fire would raise their spirits. But his hand froze mid-reach. There was only one block left. They were going to need it later.

They waited for what felt like hours—till the drowned finally stopped banging on the glass. Till quiet filled the house.

"I think they're gone," Asher whispered. "I'm going to go check."

As he hopped up from his chair, Mason grabbed

the back of his shirt. "Wait! I'll go with you." He felt Luna close behind, too, as they tiptoed down the hall.

Darkness had fallen. Had the drowned swam toward the water's surface, hoping to find new prey?

Mason scanned the glass, waiting for his eyes to adjust. At first, he saw nothing—nothing but a clump of sea grass waving side to side in the water. Then he saw two pricks of light.

He watched them bobble closer. The blue flecks grew wider, till they were pressed against the glass. And then Mason knew.

The drowned were coming back.

Thump. Thump. Thump.

When Luna cried out, Mason whirled around. "It's alright!" he said. "They can't get to us."

But Luna wasn't looking at the drowned. She was looking down. She pointed toward the sea grass on the other side of the glass.

Except now that Mason looked again, he saw more clearly. It wasn't sea grass at all.

It was tentacles. The tentacles of a squid.

Edward was on the other side of the glass, trying to get in.

Away from the drowned.

CHAPTER 8

"Will the drowned hurt Edward?"

Asher knelt near the window, reaching for the squid as if trying to help him step through the glass.

Luna answered quickly, her voice tight. "I don't know. But they attack baby turtles, so . . . he's not safe out there."

Edward's eyes widened, as if he had heard her. He raised another tentacle and pressed it to the glass, holding on for dear life.

"That's it," said Luna. "I'm going out to get him." She was already pulling on her boots.

"I'll go with you!" said Asher.

"No you won't," said Mason, pulling him back. He cared about Edward, but he cared about Asher way more.

Luna nodded. "Mason's right. I've got this. You just stay by the door, ready for me to hand Edward over. Got it?"

When Asher finally agreed, Mason blew out a breath of relief.

Luna tightened her helmet and reached for her trident. Then she stepped out through the first door, flinging it shut behind her.

Mason waited to hear the sound of the second door opening, and then he counted down from ten. *Ten, nine, eight* . . . The sponge mat would be soaking up the water now. *Seven, six, five* . . . Was Luna alright? He fought the urge to run to the window to see. *Four, three, two* . . . He flung the door open, letting just a little bit of water gush inside.

Asher followed him into the flush entrance. Then they shut the door to the living room and waited for Luna's knock on the outer door.

"C'mon!" cried Mason. "Where is she?"

When Asher reached for the handle, Mason swatted his hand away. "Not yet. Wait till she knocks."

But would she ever knock?

Mason pressed his ear to the door, trying to hear. He might as well have stuck his ear in a nautilus shell. All he heard was the hum of the ocean, a sound so familiar that he could barely hear it at all.

"What's she doing out there?" cried Asher.

"Hopefully saving a squid," said Mason. He began to pace, but the room was so small, he could take only two steps before turning around. *C'mon, Luna. Knock already!*

Then she did—a pounding so loud and furious that Mason jumped. He flung open the door without thinking, without even grabbing his weapon.

The wall of water hit first, and then a tangle of wet tentacles. Luna shoved Edward into Mason's arms and pushed her way in behind him.

When the outer door slammed shut, Mason felt a tingle of relief run from his head to his toes. But he couldn't see a thing. He pulled a sticky tentacle off his face.

"Edward, get off me!" he cried, sucking in a mouthful of water.

It took forever to stop coughing. Forever for the water level to slowly sink, and for Edward to slink down to the floor after it.

"He needs water," said Luna.

"Huh?" asked Mason, trying to wipe the slimy feeling of squid off his face.

"Edward," she said sadly. "We can keep him safe from the drowned, but he needs water to live. He can't stay in a dry place for too long."

"Now you tell me!" said Mason. "So what do we do?"

Edward had plastered himself to the wet sponge at their feet, as if it were the last puddle of water in a dry desert.

"We don't dry out the sponge, for starters," said Luna. "And then we put our heads together and try to come up with a way out of this mess."

Mason sighed as he pushed open the door to the living room. When water spilled in, he didn't try to mop it up.

As he glanced toward the glass, he did a double take.

A curtain of darkness had fallen where the drowned had stood only minutes ago.

"Are they gone?" he asked. "Did you fight them off?"

Luna shook her head. "Edward did," she said.

"How?" asked Mason, picturing Edward holding eight tiny tridents in his eight long tentacles.

"Ink," said Luna. "He squirted a cloud of ink—like the stuff you have all over your face right now."

Asher laughed out loud, pointing. "You do!" he said. "You should see it!"

But Mason didn't have to look. He'd been inked by Edward before. "Great," he murmured. "Perfect. Thanks, Edward. Thanks, buddy, old pal."

He tried to laugh, but it came out more like a squawk.

Because now I'm not just worried about myself and Asher, Mason realized. *Now I have to find a way to keep a squid alive, too.*

* * *

"What day is it?" Asher asked. "I think I'm starving to death." He flung the back of his hand to his forehead, as if he were about to faint.

"It's the same day," Luna said. "And don't be so dramatic."

Mason couldn't blame Asher. It *did* feel as if they'd been stuck inside for days. His own stomach grumbled in protest. "I think we should eat something," he finally announced. "Maybe we can split a piece of cod and save the other one for later."

"Or dry some kelp?" Asher asked hopefully.

Mason shook his head. "We can't waste fuel by smelting kelp. But you can have some *fresh* kelp if you'd like."

Asher wrinkled his nose. "Yeah, no thanks."

Mason pulled a cod fillet from the supply chest. It looked so small. Had it shrunk since he'd last checked?

As he set the cod on a plate, his mouth watered. He carefully cut the cod into three small pieces, and then slid two of them onto plates for Luna and Asher.

"What about Edward?" Luna asked, as if the squid were sitting right there at the table with them.

Mason sighed—and reached into the supply chest for the last piece of cod. He handed it to Luna, who disappeared into the other room to feed Edward.

Mason ate his cod in a single bite, but instantly, his stomach rumbled for more.

"You sound hungry," said Asher. "How about some fresh kelp?" He raised an eyebrow and smirked.

Mason sighed again—and reached into the supply chest for a few kelp leaves. As he placed the first piece on his tongue, he nearly gagged. It was so bitter! But he forced himself to chew. "Mmm . . ." he said. "Delicious."

Asher rolled his eyes. As soon as he looked away, Mason spit the green gob into his napkin. *Ew.*

When Luna returned, she was still holding the hunk of fish. "Edward won't eat," she said, her face drooping. "I'm really worried about him."

"I'm really worried about *us,*" said Mason. "All we have left for food is kelp. How long are the drowned going to hang around?"

Luna shrugged. "I don't know. But at this rate, they might outlast us—and Edward." She nibbled nervously on a fingernail. "There's no other solution. I have to go for help."

"What?" asked Mason, louder than he'd intended. "You can't go anywhere. We're surrounded!" But then curiosity got the better of him. "Besides, who would you go to for help? We're alone down here!"

Luna shook her head. "Not totally."

Huh? Mason studied her face for clues. Did she have a friend down here that he didn't know about?

"Ms. Beacon?" Asher blurted.

"No way," said Mason, remembering the woman's cold stare. "She's no friend."

He waited for Luna to agree, but she didn't. "She brews some wicked potions," said Luna. "I'll bet she could help us fight the drowned."

"I'll bet she has the heart of the sea in her treasure chest," said Asher. "We could sure use that right about now."

Luna shot him a glance. "It's not a treasure chest," she said. "It's a loot chest. It's different."

Asher stuck out his chin, refusing to listen.

"I don't want you to go," Mason said to Luna. "We'll figure out a different plan. We need to stick together."

But Luna only shrugged.

When she went to check on Edward, Mason watched her closely. When Luna had her mind set on something, it was tough to talk her out of it.

He followed her into the main room, noticing that the sun had begun to brighten the ocean floor. But the drowned were still outside the window, tall green mobs wiggling like stalks of rotten sea grass. Mason's stomach clenched. *Don't look at them,* he told himself as he quickly crossed the room.

When Luna grabbed her turtle helmet, he blocked her path. "You can't go!" he said, holding up his hand.

Luna pulled her dark hair into a ponytail beneath her helmet. "I'm just letting in some water for Edward," she said. "I'll open the door a crack, and I've got my trident to keep the drowned out. Don't worry—I know what I'm doing."

Mason glanced at the squid. Edward hugged the sponge carpet, which now looked dry as a bone. "Alright," said Mason. "But just a crack. The drowned are right outside the door."

Luna nodded and tightened her helmet. Then she stepped out of the living room and into the flush entrance with Edward.

Mason listened for the sound of the outer door clicking open. When it did, he heard water pouring in. And then the slam of the outer door again.

He counted to ten, waiting for the sponge to soak up the water—for Edward to get his fix of the wet stuff. But after ten seconds, and then twenty, and then thirty, Luna still hadn't come back in.

"Is Edward okay?" Mason hollered through the door.

There was no response. He opened the door an inch, making sure the water level had fallen. Edward had plumped back up again. He blinked contentedly at Mason from his spot on the bloated carpet.

But Luna was nowhere to be found.

CHAPTER 9

"I can't believe she left us!" cried Mason as he paced the living room, end to end.

Asher stared out the window, as if trying to catch a glimpse of Luna swimming away. But as he looked out, the drowned looked in. One began banging his mottled head against the glass.

Thump, thump, thump.

"Asher, get away from the window," Mason ordered. He didn't have to tell his brother twice. Asher took a giant step backward.

"Luna didn't *leave* us," he pointed out. "She's going for help!"

"Help from a crazy old lady who lives in a cave?" cried Mason. As soon as he'd said the words, he was glad Luna hadn't heard them. "Well, I don't know if she's crazy, but I know she's not friendly. She practically chased us out of her home."

Asher nodded. "True. But she was pretty scary. If we're fighting the drowned, I want her on my side."

Mason couldn't argue with that. He started pacing again, until the throng of drowned outside the window began to grow. "Let's get back to the furnace room," he said to Asher. "The longer we're in here, the more riled up the drowned get. It's better when they can't see us."

And when we can't see them, he thought.

But being in the furnace room only reminded Mason that they were nearly out of food, and had just one block of dried kelp left for fuel. If Luna couldn't find help, they'd never make it.

I know what I'm doing, Luna had said just before leaving.

I hope so, thought Mason. *I really hope so.*

Then he heard a yelp from the living room.

"Asher!" Mason practically flew down the hall.

His brother stood in the middle of the room. He looked unharmed, but he was pointing at the glass.

Mason turned slowly, afraid of what he might see.

The drowned were still there, but . . . he'd already known that. Why was Asher so freaked out?

"It's leaking," Asher whispered.

Mason looked again—and saw a trickle of water running down the wall. He followed the trail backward, up toward the ceiling. One of the blocks in the wall looked bloated with water. It bulged, threatening to burst out of its glass frame.

It was the block Asher had replaced, the block that had once been prismarine. But now?

It was sandstone. Very wet, very crumbly sandstone.

It looked as if a single blow with a fist could break that block to pieces.

"No," Mason breathed, shaking his head side to side. "This isn't good. This isn't good at all!" If that block crumbled, not only would water gush in, but the drowned could get in, too!

"What do we do?" asked Asher.

"We have to fix it," said Mason. But with what? He flew around the room, searching.

Could they plug the hole with the sponge from the entryway? Nope, it was too big. And Edward was hugging the sponge as if it were his new best friend.

"Here!" shouted Asher from the furnace room.

Mason raced toward his brother, feeling the eyes of the drowned on him with every step. Were they waiting for the sandstone block to break? For their chance to get inside?

He ran faster.

Asher stood beside the furnace, holding the block of dried kelp.

"That's our fuel!" said Mason.

Asher nodded. "Yeah, but it's the right size—and kind of squishy. You used one to block the hole before, remember?"

Yeah, after you broke the glass wall, Mason wanted to say. But he didn't. Because he could hear the trickle of water running down the living room wall, and it was starting to sound more like a stream.

"Grab your pickaxe," he said. "Let's go."

In the living room, Mason rushed toward the glass

wall. "We have to be quick," he said to Asher. "You break the sandstone, and I'll stick the dried kelp in its place."

Asher nodded, but his expression was grave.

"On the count of three," said Mason. "One, two . . . three!"

Asher broke the sandstone with a single blow, and Mason pushed the dried kelp into the wall. The raging water tried to push it back into the room, but Mason pushed harder.

His arms shook as he leaned against the wall, waiting for the kelp block to expand with water. Finally, he could take his hands away, and the block stayed put.

But water was *everywhere.*

"Grab the sponge!" he called to Asher. "Let's mop this up."

"Yeah, right," said Asher. "*You* grab it." He pointed toward Edward, who now had all eight tentacles wrapped around the sponge.

Mason sighed. "Edward, you're going to have to share."

But the squid wouldn't let go. When Mason reached for the corner of the sponge, the squid opened his mouth, showing off his sharp little teeth.

"I'm not scared of you," said Mason, even though he kind of was.

He reached for the other side of the sponge and started to drag it into the living room, wiping up the soppy mess. But the sponge was so full of water, it only made the mess worse.

"We have to dry it out in the furnace," said Mason. "C'mon, Edward. Let go!" He tugged the sponge across the floor, with Edward going along for the ride.

Then Mason remembered something. They couldn't dry out the sponge in the furnace, because they couldn't *light* the furnace. They had just used their last block of fuel to plug the glass wall!

He slumped down beside Edward on the floor. Cool water seeped through his jeans, but he didn't even care.

Asher shot his brother a nervous glance. "Don't worry," he said. "Luna's still out there. She's getting help, remember?"

Mason nodded. But how much help was Luna actually bringing back? She'd need a whole *army* of Ms. Beacons to fight the drowned that were clustered around their underwater home.

Mason rested his chin on Edward's wet head and sighed—until a flurry of activity on the other side of the glass caught his eye.

Something was moving through the mass of green mobs. They grunted and snarled, falling away from the glass. A trident flashed. Was it Luna?

Yes! Mason caught sight of her red shirt and dark ponytail. She battled fiercely, swinging over and over again. But did she have any help?

Mason strained to see. When he saw the white robes swirling in the water above, he knew Ms. Beacon had come, too. Her long grey hair streamed out behind her as she dove toward the drowned, toward Luna.

But as the crowd of drowned surged forward, Luna got squished up against the glass. Her trident was knocked from her hands. Hand over hand, Luna began to inch her way toward the front door.

Then a drowned threw a trident of its own. The three-pronged weapon spun through the water and knocked Luna sideways.

"No!" cried Mason, leaping from the floor. He ran to the glass, wanting to smash it to pieces and save Luna.

But it was too late.

The life drained from her eyes . . . and then she fell.

CHAPTER 10

Mason didn't reach for his helmet.

He didn't put on armor, or take a swig of potion.

He grabbed only his trident before flying out the double doors. As the water surged inward, he pushed his way out, with only one thought on his mind. *Luna.*

He struck the first drowned he came across—struck it with such rage that the beast fell backward, taking two more drowned with it.

Mason fought his way through the crowd, battling with fury, until he reached Luna's side. He grabbed her arm and pulled, straight through the crowd, waving his trident wildly with his other hand to clear a path.

As a drowned staggered backward, Mason caught sight of Ms. Beacon hovering overhead. They locked eyes for only a moment, and then she darted away like a nervous fish.

Mason didn't have time to call after her. *Save Luna,* he urged himself. *Get her to the door!*

Asher was already waiting, the door wide open. He helped Mason pull Luna inside. With his last ounce of strength, Mason swung the heavy door shut.

He waited for the water level to sink, for the entryway to clear so that he could help Luna. So that he could finally breathe.

Then he remembered. There was no sponge in here to soak up the water. He'd left that sponge in the living room with Edward!

Asher must have had the same thought. He was already pressing on the inner door. As it gave way, a wave of water gushed into the living room, taking the boys—and Luna—with it.

Mason struggled to regain his footing as he sucked in a sweet breath of air. Then he dropped to Luna's side in the knee-high water.

She lay motionless, face down. He rolled her onto her side and patted her back, willing her to breathe.

But she didn't make a sound. She didn't move at all—not even the slightest flutter of her eyelids.

"We need her potion of healing!" Asher cried. He tugged Luna's backpack off her shoulder and rummaged around inside, grabbing the first bottle he could find.

But the thin bottle looked so strange. It wasn't round and squat like Luna's other bottles, and the cork was black instead of orange. "What is this?" he asked, about to uncork the bottle.

"Wait!" said Mason, spinning the bottle until they could see the handwritten label. "Potion of weakness" was scrawled in tiny, spidery letters.

"Ms. Beacon!" he suddenly remembered. "Luna must have gotten it from her. But don't open it. That won't help Luna."

He patted Luna's face, but her body hung limp in his arms. A cold trickle of dread ran down Mason's spine.

Asher reached into the backpack and pulled out two more tall, thin bottles. "Potions of regeneration and . . . strength," he read off the labels. "Where's potion of healing?"

He dug deeper and produced a few lumps of coal and then some wheat. Luna had definitely visited Ms. Beacon, and the old woman had shared some supplies.

Finally, Asher pulled a vial of pink liquid from the depths of Luna's pack. "This is it! Splash potion of healing," he announced. "It's what she used to heal my arm."

In an instant, he had uncorked the bottle and dribbled the liquid onto Luna's face.

They watched and waited.

Please wake up, Mason prayed. *Please!*

But Luna didn't stir.

Asher opened the bottle again and poured more potion, swinging the bottle back and forth across Luna's body until every ounce was gone. "Why isn't it working?" he cried.

"Maybe it takes time," said Mason quietly.

Edward had crept closer now in the sea of water filling the living room. He watched Luna with his wide-set eyes.

"We're trying to save her, buddy," Mason told him. "We're doing the best we can!"

He wished Edward would look away. He wished the drowned outside the glass would, too. He wished the whole Overworld would go away for just a moment, long enough for Luna to get better.

But Mason could wish all he wanted. The drowned weren't going away. They were spread thick against the glass, blocking out the midday light filtering down from the sky above.

Then they began to bump and bobble against the glass.

Thump, thump, bump.

"Stop!" Mason cried out loud. "Why won't they stop?"

Asher jumped back, as if surprised by Mason's voice. "Should we fight them with Ms. Beacon's potions?" he asked.

Mason shook his head. "No way. Not without Luna. She's the only one who knows how potions work on the drowned—which ones hurt them and which ones only make them stronger."

But Luna still lay cold as a fish in his arms.

"Let's move her into the furnace room," he suddenly decided.

The furnace was cold to the touch, but the room was still warmer than the rest of the house. And there, Luna could rest away from the watchful eyes of the undead mobs glued to the windows.

As Mason and Asher carried Luna across the room, the drowned banged against the glass.

Thump, thump, bump.

In the furnace room, Mason spread a blanket over the supply chest. The chest made a nice bed, a place where Luna could lie high above the water flooding the floor.

She looked so peaceful, as if she were only fast asleep. *So that's what I'm going to pretend,* thought Mason as he and Asher pulled the door shut behind them.

Back in the living room, Mason paced furiously through the lake that had formed there. "Now what?" he said. "We don't have food. We don't have fuel. We don't have Luna. We don't have a plan!"

Asher held up his hand. "Stop pacing," he said. "And stop hollering. You're freaking me out."

Mason stopped. "Sorry. But I think it's pretty much time to freak out, don't you?"

Asher shrugged. "Maybe I can go find Ms. Beacon. Maybe I can find the heart of the sea, and finish the conduit, and . . ."

"Forget the dumb conduit!" Mason cried.

Asher took a step backward. "Uncle Bart wouldn't let you say that," he said, a wounded look creeping across his face.

Mason took a deep breath and blew it back out. "You're right. Uncle Bart wouldn't let me say that. He was always after treasure, just like you. But look where that got him!"

As soon as he'd said the words, Mason wished he could take them back. Asher's face fell, but only for a moment. Then he fought back.

"You'll see!" he said. "I'll get the heart of the sea. And

when I finish the conduit, you won't need weapons or splash potions or anything. My conduit will fight those green hunks of rotten flesh all by itself." He pointed toward the window, where the drowned wriggled and writhed.

But something else was out there now.

Mason strained to see.

"Is that . . . a zombie?" he asked. In its tattered red shirt, the mob stood out like a tropical fish against the brown robes of the drowned. But its eyes were just as cold and hollow.

The zombie let out a groan—a groan Mason could actually hear. Then it staggered forward, as if it were coming right through the glass!

Mason's jaw dropped, his mind scrambling to make sense of what he was seeing. But as the zombie's image swirled and faded, he realized—he wasn't staring at a zombie on the other side of the glass. He was staring at a reflection . . .

. . . of a zombie right here in the living room.

Mason spun so fast, he almost lost his footing. He locked eyes with the undead mob. There was no time to figure out how the zombie had gotten inside. There was barely enough time to act.

As the zombie snarled and stepped toward him, Mason grabbed his trident. He raised it over his shoulder like a spear.

"Stop!" Asher suddenly cried. "Don't strike!"

His next few words hung in the air like lingering potion.

"It's not a zombie. It's Luna!"

CHAPTER 11

Luna?

Mason searched the zombie's eyes and saw nothing familiar. But the T-shirt was hers. The tattered leggings were hers. And the boots, burst open at the seams, glowed with the faint purple of depth strider enchantment.

Yes, this was Luna.

Mason nearly ran to her side.

But this Luna wasn't a friend. *This* Luna snarled again. She wanted to harm him.

Mason used his trident to push her back, away from Asher. She stumbled backward, grunting, toward the furnace-room door.

With a final shove, Mason knocked her into the room. As she landed with a splash on the waterlogged floor, he swung the door shut and locked it.

Mason leaned against the door, trying to catch his breath. Would it be strong enough to hold her?

Asher's face held a thousand questions. "How did she turn into a zombie?" he cried, his eyes wide.

Mason shook his head. "I don't know." Then he remembered Luna's words—what she had said about Ms. Beacon way back when, before the drowned had come and their world had turned upside down.

Ms. Beacon knows how to cure a zombie villager—a villager who is killed by a zombie or a drowned, but then turns into a zombie herself.

"Luna isn't a zombie," Mason suddenly realized. "She's a zombie villager. And Ms. Beacon knows how to cure her!"

Asher spun around so fast, his feet nearly slipped out from beneath him. "Then we have to get Ms. Beacon!"

"You're not going out there," Mason said quickly. The thought of losing Asher, too—of his brother turning into a zombie villager—was way too much for Mason to bear. "We'll wait for her to come back."

Asher hesitated. "But . . . will she come back?"

Mason thought of the way Ms. Beacon had disappeared the moment he'd spotted her. But she had come to help, hadn't she? She had given Luna potions. And she had seen how badly injured Luna was.

"She'll come back," said Mason, sounding more sure than he felt. "She'll bring a cure for Luna."

Asher shook his head. "No, she won't. She doesn't even know Luna turned into a zombie!"

In an instant, Mason knew Asher was right. As Luna began to scratch at the door behind him, he jumped to his feet and began to pace. "We need to find a way to tell her," he said. "We have to send a message to Ms. Beacon." But how?

Mason imagined sending Edward, with an SOS scrawled across his shiny black head. But Luna would never forgive them if something happened to Edward.

"I know!" Asher held up a hand to stop Mason's pacing. "We'll write it on the window!" he cried.

He raced toward the living room so fast that Mason had no choice but to follow. He glanced backward, hoping that the locked furnace-room door would hold Luna safely inside. Then he sloshed through the water until he reached Asher, who had grabbed Luna's backpack. Asher pulled out the lump of coal. "We can write with this," he said.

"Write on what?" asked Mason.

Asher gestured toward the window. "On the glass."

Mason slowly nodded. "That could work! But write your message up high, where Ms. Beacon will be able to see it." *Above the drowned,* he wanted to add.

Asher pounded on the glass to force the drowned to take a step back. Then he stood on a chair, reaching upward, and began to write in thick black lines:

Luna turned into a zombie villager—please help

Mason cleared his throat. "Asher," he said, "you kind of forgot something."

Asher stepped backward to check his work. "Right." He reached up and added an exclamation point—and then another.

"No," said Mason. "You have to write backward!"

"Huh?"

"Ms. Beacon can't read that from the outside," Mason explained. "You have to write it backward!"

"Oh!" Asher's shoulders slumped.

"I'll help you." As Mason reached for the wet sponge, Edward tugged back—only a little—before dropping back down into the water that had flooded the living room floor.

With the sponge, Mason wiped the glass clean. Then he grabbed the coal, trying to ignore the drowned that was studying him through what suddenly felt like a very thin wall of glass.

Mason wrote the message, backward this time, with not two exclamation marks but three. He underlined the word *help*. Then he stood back. "How's that?" he asked.

"Genius," said Asher. "I sure hope it works."

Me too, thought Mason, tossing Edward back his sponge.

That's when he heard the scratching on the furnace-room door.

"Luna wants out," said Asher, his eyes wide. He started back down the hall.

"Don't open that door!" Mason warned him. "That's not Luna in there, not right now. She's a hostile mob. She'd rather hurt you than help you."

Asher's face fell. He stood in the hall, halfway between Mason and their friend in the furnace room, who wasn't really their friend anymore.

It's not Luna, Mason reminded himself. But his

own heart squeezed. Would they ever see Luna, the real Luna, again?

Please, Ms. Beacon, he thought, squeezing his eyes shut. *Please come back! Please help us!*

* * *

Day turned to night.

"Ms. Beacon isn't coming," said Asher. "It's night-time. There's no way she'll come now!"

Mason agreed, but said nothing. Even if Ms. Beacon did brave the journey here at night, it was so pitch-black outside, she'd never see the coal-black letters scrawled across the glass.

The only light came from the sea lantern stuck into the side of Asher's half-built conduit frame. Mason could barely see the light through the throng of drowned outside the window. But he searched for any glimmer of it, and stared at it long after Asher had fallen asleep in the chair.

I should have helped him build it! thought Mason. *We should have looked harder for the heart of the sea. If we'd finished making the conduit, we wouldn't be in this mess.*

Regret squeezed his stomach, and then hunger.

He flashed back to the shipwreck, the home he and Asher had shared on the beach before following Luna to the ocean floor. They'd been hungry then, too. They'd been fighting mobs every night, and barely sleeping. And they'd felt very much alone.

Just like now, thought Mason. He'd thought that moving underwater would make things better, that they'd be safer. *But I was wrong!* he realized now. *Dead wrong.*

He had somehow led his little brother straight back into danger.

As the clock crept into the wee hours of morning, Mason began to pace. He could barely feel his feet now, numb from the ice-cold water filling the house. But he kept walking, from one side of the room to the other.

With every step, he seemed to waken the drowned outside the window. They crept closer, crawling on top of one another to get to him—to find a way inside.

The mass was growing thicker and taller. One of the drowned had crawled upon another, reaching toward the roof of the house. Reaching toward the dried kelp block—the one block that wasn't glass—as if it were an entryway.

Then the pounding began again.

Thump, thump, thump.

Mason squeezed his eyes shut and covered his ears. *Stop!* he wanted to scream. But he couldn't wake Asher. Not when his brother was finally sleeping.

Thump, thump, thump.

Mason stepped toward the window, searching for the drowned that was banging against the glass. *Stop!* He stared at the mobs, daring them to make another sound.

Thump, thump, thump.

But the noise wasn't coming from the glass window.

Mason spun his head around. Was it Luna, in the furnace room? He covered the length of the hallway in a few quick strides, but the furnace room was silent.

Thump, thump, thump.

Am I losing my mind? wondered Mason.

He raced back into the living room, stumbling over Edward, who floated near the front door. The squid seemed to be sleeping, hugging his sponge like a security blanket.

Thump, thump, thump.

Realization struck Mason like a lightning bolt.

The banging was coming from the front door. And it wasn't banging at all. It was *knocking.* Had someone finally come to help?

CHAPTER 12

Knock, knock, knock!

Mason raced into the entryway. He reached for the handle of the outer door, about to fling it open and let the visitor inside.

Stop! screamed the voice in his head. *You don't know who this is. It could be a friend, or it could be an enemy—a clever mob, or a griefer, or . . .*

He shook his head to clear it. Then he hurried back into the living room to grab his trident and his turtle helmet. When he was suited up, he stepped into the entryway and closed the door securely behind him.

Whatever stood on the other side of the outer door, Mason was ready. He wouldn't let them in. He *had* to keep Asher safe.

He took a deep breath and opened the door, bracing himself for the wall of water. It came, nearly knocking him backward. But as Mason struggled to stand in the churning water, he saw nothing. No friend. No foe. No Ms. Beacon. No mob.

I'm too late! Mason realized. Had Ms. Beacon been knocking and finally given up?

Mason wanted to give up, too—to drop his weapon and sink to his knees in the sand and gravel. But as the drowned began to stagger toward him, he thought of Asher and of Luna, locked in that furnace room.

I'm their only hope, he realized. *I can't quit now!*

So Mason fought. He swung his trident to push the mobs back. Then he reached for the heavy door to pull it closed.

But it wouldn't budge! Something was in the way.

Mason bent low, frantically trying to clear the sea grass or kelp that was blocking the path of the door. But he found none of those things.

Instead, he saw a round package wrapped in kelp leaves and tied with a blade of sea grass. He grabbed the package, quick as lightning, and darted back inside the door.

This time, he didn't wait for the sponge mat to soak up the water. He opened the inner door and let the wave of water carry him inside. It dumped him in the middle of the living room with such a splash that Asher woke up, rubbing his eyes.

"What happened?" he asked, jumping out of the chair.

Mason held up the package. "We had a visitor," he announced. "Ms. Beacon, I think." As he began to unwrap the kelp leaves, Asher half-waded, half-swam to his side.

Asher sucked in his breath. "It's round," he

whispered. "Like the heart of the sea. I think it's the heart of the sea!" He grabbed at the package, knocking the contents out of Mason's hands.

But it wasn't a heart of the sea. It was an apple. A *golden* apple.

The fruit bobbed in the water. As Edward reached for it with a long black tentacle, Mason gently pushed him away. "No, Edward. This isn't for you. I think it's for Luna."

Sure enough, the package held a note. A few words were scrawled in Ms. Beacon's spidery handwriting:

Splash potion of weakness + golden apple

"We have the apple, but where's the splash potion?" Mason asked, checking the water at his feet. Had it fallen out?

While Asher swam in a circle, bobbing his head underwater in search of the missing potion, Mason smoothed out the packaging in his hands to be sure the bottle wasn't hidden inside. Then he remembered. Ms. Beacon had already given Luna the potion of weakness. It was in her backpack!

He reached for her pack and dug through the contents, trying not to break the glass bottles. The potion of weakness was at the very bottom. He held the purple liquid up to the light of the sea lantern.

Thump, thump, thump!

The drowned had begun to bang again on the glass window. The noise grew louder, angrier.

"They're mad," said Asher. "You made them mad by going outside."

As the brothers watched, the drowned began to push against the glass, climbing one upon another.

"Is the wall shaking?" asked Asher.

Mason felt it, too—a vibration that sent the water on the floor rippling. He stared at the glass wall, his eyes zeroing in on the dried kelp block near the top. One of the drowned was only inches away from that block. Would it keep the drowned out? Was it strong enough?

He gripped the potion in his hand. "Grab the apple!" he called to Asher.

Together, they raced down the hall toward the furnace room. Mason pressed his ear to the door. He heard nothing but silence.

"Is she sleeping?" Asher whispered.

"I don't know," said Mason. "Do zombie villagers sleep?"

They were about to find out.

"Here's the plan," said Mason, trying to keep his voice steady. "You open the door, and I'll throw the potion. Then you roll the apple inside, and we'll pull the door shut. Got it?"

Asher nodded solemnly. He was gripping the golden apple so tightly, his knuckles had turned white.

"Ready?" asked Mason, his heart pounding in his ears.

"Ready," Asher whispered.

"Now!"

As Asher flung open the door, Mason scanned the room for Luna. There she was, crouched by the furnace. She stared back with eyes so cold and empty that Mason felt the hair stand up on his arms.

Before she could make a move, he threw the bottle. It smashed on the floor inches in front of Luna, the purple liquid splattering her tattered clothes.

"Roll the apple!" cried Mason.

Asher did.

It bounced once, twice, and then rolled to a stop beside Luna. She barely flinched.

Then Mason pulled the door shut. When he heard the *click* of the lock, he finally released the breath he'd been holding.

Asher's face was white as a ghast. "Now what?" he asked.

Mason shrugged. "Now we wait." Ms. Beacon hadn't told them how long it took for the cure to work—or even how likely it was to work at all. *But it has to work,* he thought. *We need Luna!*

The drowned were still thumping against the glass. Mason could feel it, even here, all the way down the hall.

He thought again of the dried kelp block—the weakest part of the wall. "C'mon," he said, leading Asher back toward the living room. As much as Mason didn't want to see the drowned, he had to keep an eye on them.

Because if that wall caves in, we're done for! he realized, his stomach clenching.

The drowned were stacked two high now, all across the wall.

"Look!" cried Asher, pointing.

A drowned was inching its way onto the roof. He hung there, writhing, like a storm cloud in the sky—dark, ugly, and threatening.

"What do we do?" asked Asher.

"What *can* we do?" said Mason. He began to pace. But as his eyes flickered back toward the glass, he saw water trickling down.

Plop, plop, plop . . .

Droplets of water dripped off the block of dried kelp. With all the thumping and bumping, the squishy block had begun to slip back into the room!

Thump, thump, thump!

A drowned banged the glass, just beneath the block of dried kelp.

"Stop him!" cried Mason. "He'll push the block right through!"

Asher stood on tiptoe to reach the block. "Help me!" he cried.

Mason was beside him in a flash. But as he squeezed his hands against the block of kelp, he came face-to-face with the drowned. The mob was inches away—staring at Mason through the glass.

Bump, bump, bump . . .

He banged his head against the glass, as if trying to strike Mason, too. Then he let out a growl, loud enough for Mason to hear from inside his water-logged home.

"Push harder!" Mason cried.

Asher responded in a squeaky voice.

"What?" asked Mason. He glanced sideways, just long enough to see that Asher wasn't looking at the glass. He was staring over his shoulder at something in the room.

But what?

Mason whirled around—and suddenly realized that Asher hadn't spoken at all. The squeaky voice had come from someone else.

"What's going on?" Luna asked again.

Luna! Mason's heart leaped at the sight of his friend.

She rubbed her face as if waking from a dream. Then her eyes widened. She sucked in her breath and pointed.

CHAPTER 13

Ccrrrackkk!

Mason spun around just in time to see the jagged line form in the glass wall behind him. It raced like a lightning bolt from the block of dried kelp toward the horde of green mobs below.

And then the glass gave way.

Water gushed toward Mason as if in slow motion.

Run! he thought to himself. But by the time his feet came unglued from the ground, there was no time to run.

There was only time to swim.

Mason dove toward Luna. He felt Asher on his heels. But as the water surged forward through the broken glass, it carried Mason across the room. *Smack!* He hit the opposite wall. The water held him there, trapped. Mason pounded on the wall with his fist, but it was too thick to break.

We have to swim the other way! he realized. *Toward the drowned.* It was the only way out. He grabbed Luna's hand and waved at Asher.

As Mason swam, he dodged the objects floating in front of him. A chair. A wooden bowl. A trident. He grabbed the trident just as something tugged at him from behind.

Luna was struggling to break free from his grip. When he saw the flash in her eyes, he knew—Luna was back, and she was ready to fight. As soon as he let go of her hand, she dove low, toward her backpack.

Asher had grabbed something too—a pickaxe. But there were no helmets within reach. Nothing to help them breathe underwater for long, except the potion in Luna's pack. Was she getting it out now? Mason wondered.

No! Luna was already swimming toward the drowned—toward a fight. But with what weapon?

Wait! Mason wanted to shout. He kicked his feet to catch up, jabbing his sharp trident forward with each stroke of his arms. He passed Luna just before she reached the first drowned.

Thwack! Mason swung his trident. *Thwack, thwack!* He began to clear a path through the drowned, knocking them left and right.

Asher was beside him now, too, brandishing his pickaxe as if it were a sword.

But as Mason swung his trident again, he hit something hard—so hard that the impact sent a ripple of pain up his arm. He cried out, releasing the breath he'd been holding.

Then he saw what he had struck—a block of prismarine, lit by the sea lantern beside it. The frame around Asher's conduit! Mason had run straight into it.

The drowned were closing in, wrapping around the prismarine frame, sucking Mason and Asher down into its center.

Then Luna pushed her way through the pack. What was in her hand? A potion bottle. Something tall and thin.

She banged it against the prismarine, over and over. Mason didn't hear the glass break, but he saw the lavender particles spill out, filling the water with a purplish haze.

As the potion reached him, Mason clamped his mouth shut. If the potion was meant to harm the drowned, would it harm him, too? He wasn't taking any chances. He clamped his hand over Asher's mouth, too.

But as the lavender cloud reached the drowned, the mobs began to fall away. Mason watched in wonder as they dropped, snarling and grunting, toward the ocean floor.

Then his lungs began to burn.

He pointed toward Luna's pack, motioning for the potion of water breathing. He patted his chest, trying to tell her. *We need to breathe!*

But Luna was distracted. What was she looking at?

Mason glanced up.

Edward! The squid's tentacles opened and closed as he pushed himself down toward Luna.

Just as the squid reached her side, something rose from the ocean floor. The drowned were getting back up. The potion was already wearing off!

Mason's lungs were on fire now.

As black spots filled the water in front of him, he fought to stay awake. *Don't let me pass out,* he prayed. *Not now. Asher and Luna need me!*

But as the world went dark, he realized: *I didn't faint. I'm awake. I'm . . . slippery.*

He rubbed at his face, his fingers smearing across the oily surface.

Oil. Squid oil.

Edward had squirted ink, trying to protect himself against the drowned.

But now none of us can see! thought Mason with horror.

He stumbled forward, trying to escape the black cloud. He pushed past the prismarine wall, tripping over the drowned that were still on the ground. He swung his arms blindly, trying to clear the air.

Finally, the darkness gave way to grey—to clearer water, and then . . . to something else.

To a door.

A wooden door, built straight into the side of a dirt mound.

Mason opened it, stepped into the dark space beyond, and fell to his knees.

CHAPTER 14

Thump! Thump!

Mason woke to a pounding noise. He sat up so quickly, his head spun.

There was Luna's worried face, floating just inches above his own. She waved a potion bottle, as if offering him a sip.

He shook his head. He didn't remember swallowing the potion of water breathing, but he must have—the taste of pufferfish lingered in his throat. Mason inhaled deeply, letting the cool water soothe his lungs.

Then he saw Asher, slowly swinging a pickaxe against the wall of dirt.

Where are we? Mason wondered, pushing himself up to sitting. Then he remembered.

The drowned had attacked. The squid had squirted ink. Mason had searched for safety and found a hut—Asher's half-built, half-baked idea of a house.

But it saved me, Mason knew. He leaned back

against the wooden door, not wanting to think about what was on the other side.

Asher was working so hard right now, but why? Was he hoping to tunnel out the other side? Mason shot Luna a questioning look.

She pointed toward the door.

Huh? Then it dawned on him. Asher was making another door, trying to build a flush entrance so that they could find a pocket of air to breathe in. But without a sponge, how would they drain the room of water?

He shook his head, trying to clear the cobwebs and think more clearly.

Then Asher stopped swinging. He used his hands to start digging through the dirt. What had he found?

From the look on Asher's face, it was something good—*really* good.

Mason leaned over to help him dig. His hands brushed against something smooth and hard, like a plank of wood. Then his fingers rounded a corner and found a smooth iron latch.

A chest. They'd found a treasure chest!

Asher yanked backward on the chest so hard, he fell. But the chest slid out of the dirt just enough for them to force open the lid.

As Mason pulled out an iron ingot, and then a gold ingot, Asher pushed his hands past Mason's to dig deeper.

He pulled out something smooth and round. Something blue as prismarine. He held it in his hands so tenderly, Mason wondered if his brother had found a baby turtle in that chest.

Then he held it out to show Mason and Luna.

Asher had found *exactly* what he'd been looking for, right here in this underwater hill.

He had found the heart of the sea.

* * *

"Let me do it!" Asher pleaded.

He stood beside Luna's crafting table, clutching the heart of the sea. Luna had already loaded up the table with spiral nautilus shells, but she stood aside so that Asher could add his newfound treasure.

Together, while Mason watched in wonder, they crafted the conduit—a speckled square block. It didn't look like much yet, but when they placed it into the prismarine frame Asher had built, the conduit would work its magic.

That's the block that's going to save us, thought Mason. *I hope!*

As he checked the windows again, he felt the hair on the back of his neck stand up. They had managed to tunnel out the other side of the dirt mound, escaping to Luna's underwater base without the drowned seeing. But any moment now, the drowned would discover them here—would surround Luna's home just as they had Mason and Asher's.

"Hurry!" he urged the others.

Luna raced toward the supply chest. As she dug out

some leather armor and turtle helmets, Mason marveled at how quickly she had recovered. Her red T-shirt was still tattered, like the clothes of a zombie, but her eyes were clear and bright.

"What?" she asked, catching him staring at her.

Mason shook his head. "Nothing," he said with a smile. "Just glad to have you back."

Luna blew the bangs off her forehead. "Me, too," she said. "But we can celebrate later. There's work to do. Take this!" She tossed him an iron sword.

Mason slid the sword into his sheath and then helped Asher lug the conduit block toward the front door. After a few sips of potion and a few deep breaths, they waited for Luna to open the door to her flush entrance.

Just like the one we used to have, thought Mason. Picturing their new glass house, destroyed, cast a shadow over him. But he shook it off. *We'll fight the drowned, and then we'll rebuild,* he promised himself.

"Ready?" asked Luna.

"Ready," said Mason, tightening his helmet.

Then they were off, swimming through the long rocky tunnel that led from the safety of Luna's home to the underwater world beyond.

The conduit was clunky, but it felt much lighter in the water. Mason and Asher swam with it between them while Luna scouted the path ahead. She had her trident drawn, ready for the drowned.

Will they still be crawling all over the ruins of our house? Mason wondered.

He didn't have to wonder for long. As they passed the dirt mound where they had discovered the heart of the sea, Mason could already see them. The drowned surrounded the glass shards of the destroyed house, staggering through it aimlessly.

But Luna's eyes weren't set on the house. She made a beeline toward the prismarine frame, the power source for the conduit they had crafted. She waved her arm over her shoulder.

Mason kicked harder, faster with his legs, as he and Asher approached the prismarine blocks. As they lowered the conduit into the center of the frame, a current tugged at the conduit, sending it crashing into the wall.

Hold it tight! Mason willed Asher with his eyes. *Don't let go!*

He used his legs to brace himself against the frame, lowering the conduit so slowly that his arms began to shake. Finally, the block had settled onto its base. Then Mason pulled Asher backward. What would happen next?

He held his breath, waiting.

At first, nothing happened. A school of tropical fish swam by. The sea grass rippled in the water. And then . . . the drowned began to come.

Out of the house, they spilled and staggered. Mason tugged Asher's hand back farther still and reached for his sword.

Not again, he thought. *We can't fight them again. This time, we may not win!*

As the first drowned approached, Mason swung his

sword. It was lighter than his trident had been, but just as powerful. The drowned snarled and swung at the weapon. Then Luna was upon it, poking it backward with her trident.

But the others were on their way, an angry mob that stretched across the ocean floor like a wriggling wall.

Mason glanced again at the conduit. *Do something!* he wanted to scream. He kicked at the prismarine frame. *Do something!*

Then suddenly, it did. The conduit began to shake. It opened up, revealing the spinning blue sphere inside. The world lit up with its glow.

As Mason swam closer, watching, he saw the drowned closest to the conduit freeze. They staggered backward. They grunted and groaned. And then they dropped, in great writhing heaps. They lay like a green blanket across the ocean floor.

He turned toward Asher. *We did it!* he wanted to holler.

His brother pumped his fist and grinned.

Then Mason caught sight of something else—someone else—swimming overhead. Luna?

No! The woman was clothed in long white robes. Her hair swirled around her as she stopped and stared.

In the glow of the conduit, Ms. Beacon looked younger somehow—friendlier. She locked eyes with Mason, only for a moment. Was that a smile stretching across her face? Yes. And then she was gone.

CHAPTER 15

Thwack! Thwack! Whack!

This time, it was Mason swinging the pickaxe at the wall of dirt. He was widening the room in the dirt mound, the place where they had found the heart of the sea.

"Is this big enough?" he asked Luna, standing back to admire his work.

"It's plenty big enough," answered Asher, barely looking up. He sat with his back against the wall, reading Uncle Bart's leather journal.

Mason sighed. "You have to help, too," he told Asher. "Rebuilding our house is going to take time, especially if we want to do it right."

Asher shrugged. "I just built the conduit that pretty much saved us. Isn't that enough help for now?"

Mason started to argue, but then changed his mind. Asher's conduit *had* pretty much saved them. So he left his brother to his reading and turned back toward the dirt wall.

"I think I'm starting to get why Ms. Beacon lives in a cave," he said to Luna.

"Why's that?" she asked as she smoothed out the wall with her hand.

"Glass walls are great," he said. "Except when you're surrounded by drowned. This time, we should make sure that part of our home is hidden."

She nodded. "Maybe you can have a little of both," she said. "Dirt walls *and* glass walls."

"Tinted-blue glass?" Mason asked. "Two blocks thick?" He grinned, remembering all of the "suggestions" Luna had had when he'd built his first house.

She laughed. "Good idea. Why didn't I think of that?"

"I have an even better idea," said Asher. He held up the journal, pointing at a sketch that Uncle Bart had drawn. "We could build a redstone circuit—an alarm that would tell us whenever the drowned started creeping around. All we need to do is find some redstone dust!"

Mason groaned. "We're not going on another treasure hunt," he said. "We have everything we need right here."

"Huh?" Asher's eyes widened. "I wasn't going to hunt for buried treasure. I was thinking about asking Ms. Beacon if she has any redstone dust."

Mason laughed with relief. "Okay, good. So you don't think she's a witch anymore?"

Asher rolled his eyes, as if that were the dumbest idea ever. "Of course not. She's our friend. She helped us save Luna, remember?"

Mason glanced at Luna. "I remember."

He also remembered how he'd felt about Ms. Beacon the first time he'd seen her—how scary she had seemed as she'd chased them from her home.

But things aren't always what they seem, he realized now. Someone who looked like a witch or a zombie might actually be a friend. And something that looked like a simple dirt mound might actually hide an underwater home—or even buried treasure, like the heart of the sea.

As Asher suited up to go visit Ms. Beacon, Mason followed him out. Their underwater base was lit by the conduit, which cast a warm blanket of light and safety across the ocean floor.

Mason spun in a circle, admiring the beauty of the underwater village. Now that the drowned were gone, the tropical fish had returned. Edward floated lazily above the coral reef. And sunlight trickled down from above, sending shimmers of light dancing through the water.

Yep. We have everything we need right here, thought Mason with a smile. *At least for now.*